To Ellie, whose imagination inspired this book

First published in 2019 by Child's Play (International) Ltd
Ashworth Road, Bridgemead, Swindon SN5 7YD, UK

First published in USA in 2019 by Child's Play Inc
250 Minot Avenue, Auburn, Maine 04210

Distributed in Australia by Child's Play Australia Pty Ltd
Unit 10/20 Narabang Way, Belrose, Sydney, NSW 2085

ISBN 978-1-78628-201-9
L161118CPL01192019

Printed in Heshan, China

1 3 5 7 9 10 8 6 4 2

A catalogue record of this book
is available from the British Library

www.childs-play.com

Where did you go today?

Jenny Duke

Guess what?

Today I flew...

...over the trees!

I climbed...

up high...

...and slid down a mountain.

I whirled round and round...

...and sailed as far as I could see.

I crawled ashore...

...through the dark and cold.

I raced...

...across a desert...

...and I zipped...

...through a jungle...

...and rode home all the way...

...to you!